Hope you enjoy my Story

Love and Purrs,

Bunny

HELLO, MY NAME IS BUNNY!

LONDON

Hello, My Name is Bunny! London

For information about this title or to order other books and/or electronic media, contact the publisher:

Positivity Publishing LLC.

bunny@hellobunnybloom.com

www.hellobunnybloom.com

@hellobunnybloom

@hellobunnybloom

@hellobunnybloom

ISBN: 978-0-9976425-4-4

Printed in the United States of America

Cover and Interior Design: 1106 Design

For ages 6+

Dedication

For Bunny and every
homeless animal awaiting
their forever home.

"Until one has loved an
animal, a part of one's soul
remains unawakened."

—ANATOLE FRANCE

Help Bunny make a difference:

For every *Hello, My Name is Bunny! London* book sold, we donate $2 to U.S. animal shelters.

Please go to www.hellobunnybloom.com for information on donation recipients.

CONTENTS

CHAPTER 1

HERE IN LONDON

Hello, my name is Bunny, and I'm a two-year-old tuxedo girl cat who's lived a life of international adventure. In fact, I'm famous for rescuing a Central Park carriage horse named Joe in New York City just last year. But you can read all about that in my first book, if you haven't already. Now I'm way on the other side of the Atlantic Ocean, in a country called England, where things *really* got interesting not long ago.

I live in Lambeth, in south London. My new home is a beautiful old townhouse with a cozy backyard protected by a brick wall and shaded by a tree that grows plums as sweet as sugar. Despite my perilous adventures in New York City last year, my human parents still let me go in the yard whenever I want to. That's where I am right now, snug in my favorite shoebox beside a patch of yellow daffodils that sprouted just last week!

During the day, my human mom, Joan, is a psychologist who helps people feel happier. And my human dad, Robert, is a diplomat who makes sure the United States and England stay friendly. I'm usually not alone while mom and dad are at work. That's because my friends Lily, Goldy, and Rocky are often around to keep me company. I'm just glad the wall separating my yard from theirs isn't too high. Otherwise I never would have met Lily, Goldy, and Rocky, and none of what I'm about to tell you would have happened!

I'll introduce you to Rocky first. He's the rather large, chubby-cheeked tabby cat belonging to the Haywards, the nice people who live next door. Rocky doesn't say or do much. He prefers to sleep, either in the plum tree or right atop the wall. I don't know why; neither looks especially comfortable or safe. But sleeping in precarious places is how the big, lazy cat passes most of his time, scarcely moving a muscle.

Next, meet Goldy, Lily's golden labrador puppy, who spends hours on end running in circles and back and forth and even in figure 8s, which can be dizzying to watch. Besides darting around with no apparent purpose, Goldy's favorite activity is chasing the orange-and-black butterflies that flap and float among the flowers Mrs. Hayward planted this spring. I'll occasionally climb over the wall and play with Goldy, but only for a while, because the little furry dynamo's too energetic, even for a frisky cat like me.

Then there's ten-year-old Lily Hayward—undoubtedly the best thing about living here. Lily's quiet and small for her age, and she occasionally ties her straight blond hair into a ponytail. This allows a better view of her moon-shaped face and her pale blue eyes, which appear to hold the knowledge and wisdom of someone much older than she is. Those wise eyes of Lily's often looked sad and worried, though, and I couldn't ignore how she would frequently sit alone in her garden for hours, seemingly deep in thought.

I should know by now that trying to help when something's wrong can be a darned good way to get in trouble. Yet, despite living in a different country and city, one thing about me that remains the same is my desire to pay forward all the good fortune I've had since being born in and rescued from a dark, dangerous Brooklyn basement. This not only motivated me to risk life and limb saving Joe the Carriage

Horse in New York City, it also inspired me to help Lily Hayward be happy instead of sad. And that's exactly what led me on an equally great adventure here in London. So stay tuned, Dear Reader, because I'm going to tell you all about it!

BUNNY

CHAPTER 2

THE MISSION

Little did I know my big London adventure would begin on such an ordinary morning several months ago. I'd been curled like a shrimp in my shoebox, which is where I do my best thinking and dreaming. Lily had come out of her house and over to the wall, the way she normally did.

"Hi, Bunny."

I aimed my big green eyes up at my neighbor.

"Hi, Lily. How are you today?"

"I'm fine."

But Lily's expression told a different story.

"Are you sure you're fine?"

"Sure, I'm sure. After all, I'm so lucky to have everything I could possibly need—a nice house and garden, loving parents, and Rocky, my good-natured cat. I also have Goldy, the cutest golden labrador puppy in the world, and my special friend, Bunny Simmons-Bloom!"

"I feel the same way about you, Lily. I'm incredibly lucky, too. For instance, when I was just a tiny kitten, I got rescued from a damp Brooklyn basement and then adopted by Joan and Robert. I even became a bit of a celebrity for saving a Central Park carriage horse. But don't get me started on that."

I stepped out of my box and jumped onto the wall beside Rocky, who'd been sleeping there the whole time.

"Yes, we're both incredibly blessed," Lily said, as if still trying to convince herself.

"Then why do you look so anxious and unhappy?" I asked.

Lily's eyes misted as she searched for words that seemed just beyond reach.

"To be honest, Bunny, some kids at school aren't always nice to me."

Nothing upsets me more than young humans or animals being mistreated.

"Care to tell me about it, Lily?"

Lily gathered her composure before describing the teasing she'd get for being skinny and shy and "nerdy." I wasn't sure what "nerdy" even meant.

"They also say I'm ugly."

I felt so shocked I couldn't speak at first.

"Ugly? Lily, you happen to be the loveliest girl I've ever met."

"You don't have to say that, Bunny."

"It's the truth."

Lily smiled through her tears.

"Thanks. I feel a little better now."

I decided then and there that my new mission would be to somehow help Lily feel a *lot* better *all* the time, not just a *little* better right *now*. But how? I considered visiting her school and asking her classmates to be nicer to her and to stop saying she's skinny and shy and ugly. I considered demanding they quit calling her "nerdy" too. I racked my brain for a better idea until it occurred to me that one of the best ways to help people is to get them to help themselves. And I truly believe the best way for someone to help themselves is by helping others. It's worked for me so far!

"Tell me, Lily, what would you like to be when you grow up?"

Lily didn't have to think for long.

"I'd like to be a veterinarian."

"Well, there's no one I'd rather have care for me than Dr. Lily Hayward if I ever get sick or injured."

"Thanks, Bunny. I do hope you never get sick or injured."

Lily's desire to help animals reminded me of an article about London foxes I'd recently read in *The Guardian* newspaper.

"Hey, Lily. Have you ever seen a fox?"

"I have. There're actually loads of them around here nowadays."

"Do they scare you?"

"Not at all. I think they're quite cute and nice. Why do you ask?"

"I ask because an article I read the other day mentioned London is planning a fox cull."

Lily looked confused. "What's a *cull*?"

I explained that a cull means killing animals on a large scale.

"That's terrible," Lily said. "Why in the world do they want to do that?"

"They say they're tipping over garbage cans and making a mess of the sidewalks and streets."

"*I* make messes sometimes," Lily said. "I don't think I should suffer for it."

"I make messes, too. More than just *sometimes*."

"There must be another reason, Bunny. It can't only be because of trash on the pavements and streets."

"There *is* another reason, I hate to say. Some people quoted in the article claim foxes are threatening small children and even pets like me and Rocky and Goldy."

Lily shook her head.

"I don't believe that."

"Neither do I."

"We have to do something about this, Bunny."

"I agree. But what?"

Lily thought for several moments.

"Perhaps we can find the leader of the foxes and talk to him."

The Haywards' back door opened before I could respond, and the little fur ball named Goldy bolted out of the house.

"Hiya, mum! Hiya, Bunny! What you guys up to? What you guys talkin' about? Can we *play*?"

Lily lifted Goldy and kissed his velvety head.

"We're talking about saving the London foxes, Goldy. Foxes are your cousins, you know."

Goldy's eyes widened.

"Foxes are my cousins?"

"Distant ones, yes. But foxes actually look and act much like you do."

Goldy's eyes brightened.

"Can I help save them, mum?"

"You just focus on being a puppy for now."

Goldy started licking Lily's face, as if on cue. Lily began to laugh, and so did I, because Goldy is perhaps the funniest creature I've ever known. Lily put him down, and the bouncy little guy immediately chased a butterfly across the yard. He soon forgot about the butterfly in favor of a robin that had landed beside Mrs. Hayward's blue tulips. He then chased his tail around and around in a circle, causing Lily and me to laugh even louder. This woke Rocky, who slowly opened his eyes and silently stared straight ahead, at nothing in particular.

"Separate bins for food," he finally muttered, in a semi-conscious state.

Lily and I looked at each other.

"'Separate bins for food'?" we both said, equally confused.

Rocky didn't elaborate or reply. He'd already shut his eyes again, and his breathing had already settled into a steady sleep rhythm.

CHAPTER 3

THE ADVENTURE BEGINS

We agreed to sneak out of our houses at midnight and meet in Lily's backyard. Our plan entailed finding the leader of the London foxes and asking him to order his foxes to stop scattering garbage and threatening children and pets. I arrived first and found Rocky still sleeping on the wall. I nudged him awake and invited him to join us. Rocky lifted his head off his paws, issued a big, toothy yawn, and told me he felt a bit too tired.

"Besides, somebody has to keep an eye on the garden," he added.

"No one can do that better than you, Rocky."

Lily appeared a minute later, wearing a knapsack and holding a leash attached to Goldy's collar.

"Do I have to be on a leash, mum?"

Lily held her finger to her lips.

"Shhh, Goldy. We don't want to wake your granny and granddad. And yes, you *do* have to be on a leash because I'm responsible for you."

"I promise I won't run off. I promise I'll be good."

"To be honest, I'd leave you here if I could be sure you wouldn't tattle on me."

Goldy stamped his paw against the ground.

"I'm *not* a tattler!"

"*Oh?* How about the time you told granny and granddad I ate that chocolate before supper?" Lily immediately softened. "Okay, you can be off the leash later on, but only if you stay by my side at all times."

Goldy began jumping up and down.

"*Yippeeee!*"

Lily shushed the tiny dog again before removing her knapsack and opening it.

"What's the knapsack for?" I asked, although I had a fairly good idea.

"To put you in, Bunny. That way I can keep you with us."

I preferred to be free and not a burden.

"I won't be too heavy for you?"

"I may be petite, but I'm strong," Lily said. "Plus, you're a rather small kitty."

True enough. I *do* weigh only eight and a quarter pounds. I reluctantly allowed Lily to put me in the knapsack. She lifted it with me inside, slipped her arms through the straps, and tightened them. She then went to the little wooden shed at the back of the yard and retrieved a cherry-red Raleigh with pink and white streamers tied to its handlebars.

"You guys ready?" she asked, wheeling her bicycle over to the iron gate that opens into a narrow alley between her house and mine.

"As ready as I'll ever be," I said, despite my sudden misgivings.

"Let's *gooooo*!" Goldy cried.

Lily leaned down and petted Goldy's head. I detected a slight quiver in her fingers when she reached back and petted mine next. Not that I blamed her for being nervous; you never know what will happen when you start on a new adventure. The thing is, Lily decided to go ahead with our plan to save the London foxes regardless of her fear and despite her trepidation. I couldn't help admiring her for that.

***

The three of us snuck out of the Haywards' backyard, leaving behind a soundly sleeping Rocky. Lily latched the gate, and I felt increasingly anxious as we headed down the alley to the sidewalk. Mainly because I knew Joan and Robert wouldn't approve of me being there, especially after I'd promised never to do anything like this again. Still, my need to help Lily and the London foxes proved even stronger than my desire to be obedient. I truly wished life would stop presenting me with such dilemmas. With only my head protruding from the knapsack, I managed to extend my neck enough to speak into Lily's ear.

"Which way should we go?" I asked her, partly because I had no idea and partly because I wanted Lily to make the decisions on this mission.

Lily brought her first knuckle to her mouth.

"Let's see. We could go toward the tube station. Or we could go the other way toward the shop where mum likes to buy groceries. Hmmm. Perhaps we should cross the street first, after looking both ways, of course."

Goldy jumped up against Lily's front tire.

"Let's gooooo, muuum!"

Lily shushed the impatient puppy once more.

"Now what did you agree to, young mister?"

Goldy lay on his belly and rested his chin on the pavement between his paws.

"I just want to have fun already," he grumbled.

"This isn't about fun, Goldy. This is about saving foxes."

I'd been looking around all the while, my keen night vision allowing me to see the houses lining the street, banged-up garbage cans in front of each. I also saw cars parked at the curb and bicycles chained to lampposts and to fences corralling small front yards. I didn't see any people, and the only sounds at first were the occasional car driving along a nearby street and a dog barking in the distance. I listened more closely and heard a TV broadcasting an old movie through an open window. I heard classical music floating through another. Nighttime London certainly looks and sounds different than daytime London; more mysterious, even a little menacing. Although I realized most of the menace lived only in my imagination.

I sensed Lily's apprehension as she tried to decide which way to go. One thing I'd learned in New York City is that taking action, some sort of action, is usually better than taking none at all. I also knew humor can be a good way to bolster someone's courage.

"Hey, Lily. Why did the girl throw the clock out the window?"

"Beats me. Why did the girl throw the clock out the window?"

"Because she wanted to see time fly."

I felt some of the tension leave Lily's body.

"Here's one, Bunny: Why did the biscuit go to the hospital?"

"I don't know. Why did the biscuit go to the hospital?"

"Because it felt crummy."

"That's funny."

Goldy piped in while I tried to remember another riddle.

"I have one. Wanna hear it?"

"I didn't know you knew any riddles, Goldy," Lily said.

"This is my favorite. What dog keeps the best time?"

Lily pinched her lower lip while pretending to think of the answer.

"A watchdog keeps the best time," Goldy said before Lily could give it. "Get it, mum? Get it, Bunny?"

Lily and I chuckled, not because it was a particularly clever riddle, but because a six month-old puppy had told it. I also believe laughing at someone's riddle or joke is the polite thing to do.

A sharp, metallic sound from across the street abruptly ended our riddle telling. Lily tensed again, and Goldy sprang to his paws.

"W-w-what was *that*?" he asked.

I squinted toward the noise and soon spotted a long, fluffy tail protruding from an overturned garbage can rolling back and forth on the pavement.

"Do you see that?" I said, aiming my paw past Lily's ear at the commotion.

"What do you think it is?" asked Lily.

I couldn't be sure until the creature in the can shimmied out, revealing itself to be a fox with reddish-gray fur, perky ears, and a black button nose. The street lamp glinted off its dark, marble-like eyes when it swung around to face us with a chicken carcass in its mouth.

"It's a fox!" I said.

Goldy began to jump up and down.

"A fox! A fox!" He looked up at Lily. "Can I go say hello to it, mum?"

"I have to make sure it's safe first, Goldy. Stay behind me, please."

Lily hesitated before stepping off the sidewalk and approaching the fox on the other side of the street.

"Do you speak English?" she asked it when she got closer.

The fox dropped the chicken.

"I didn't steal the chicken. I swear—I found it in the trash."

Lily breathed a sigh of relief that the fox seemed friendly enough. I remained vigilant.

"I'm not concerned about the chicken," Lily said. "Actually, I *am* concerned about the chicken. Because foxes eating chickens and such from rubbish bins is one reason humans are planning to kill them."

"So I've heard," the fox said. "But how else would we get enough to eat?"

"My mum here feeds me every morning and every night," Goldy said. "Sometimes my granny and granddad feed me in the afternoon while mum's at school. I'd be happy to share my food with you."

The fox smiled at Goldy.

"That's very kind and generous of you."

I leaned toward Lily's ear again.

"Ask him his name," I whispered.

Lily nodded.

"Um, tell me, fox. What's your name?"

"It's Freddy Fox."

"Freddy Fox is a good name for a fox. My name's Lily Hayward."

"Lily Hayward's a good name for a human."

"Now ask him to take us to his leader," I whispered.

"So, um, Freddy Fox, we were thinking we'd, um, we'd like to meet your leader, if possible. The leader of the London foxes."

I'd noticed Freddy Fox glancing at the chicken every so often. I preferred that to him glancing at me.

"Why do you want to meet my leader?"

Lily hesitated before saying, "I just think we could tell him— "

"It's a *her*."

"I just think we could tell *her* that not all humans want to kill foxes, and maybe we can find a way to prevent the cull that's been planned."

Freddy Fox seemed to forget about the chicken while he considered Lily's proposal.

"I don't think that's such a good idea," he said. "Chieftess Fox doesn't like humans or dogs. She's not crazy about cats, either."

"I bet we can change her mind," I said.

"I doubt that."

"Well, the only way to find out is for you to take us to her."

Freddy Fox seemed unable to refute my reasoning.

"I *could* take you to Chieftess Fox's headquarters," he said. "The problem is I can't guarantee she'd see you, and you'd have to promise not to tell anyone where her headquarters is."

"I promise," Lily said.

"Me, too!" Goldy said.

"What about you, little cat?"

"I have a name, you know. It's 'Bunny.'"

"'Bunny's an odd name for a cat. Although you *do* have big ears, like a bunny."

"I also like to hop sometimes. It's lots of fun and good exercise."

"Do you promise not to tell anyone where Chieftess Fox's headquarters is, Bunny?"

"I won't say a word."

This seemed to satisfy Freddy Fox.

"Okay, then. Follow me."

Our new friend turned and started down the sidewalk. Lily climbed onto her bicycle and began to pedal after him while Goldy trotted beside us. I didn't have to do anything except stay cocooned in the knapsack as we headed off into London with no idea what awaited us. Anything could have happened from then on, and that's what worried me, Dear Reader. Because *I'm* the one who'd given Lily the idea to help the London foxes. Which meant *I'd* be responsible if something went wrong.

CHAPTER 4

JOURNEY TO HYDE PARK

London is much like New York City in that it never truly sleeps. Which is exactly what I felt like doing while zipped in Lily's knapsack, increasingly drowsy from the gentle swaying of her bicycle. Goldy tried his best to stay beside us as we followed Freddy Fox toward Chieftess Fox's headquarters, but he couldn't help stopping to sniff fire hydrants and trash bins and trees growing from the sidewalks. He even paused to pee against one of those metal newspaper dispensers.

"You must keep up, Goldy!" Lily said.

"Okay, mum, but there's so much stuff to sniff and pee against out here."

"You can sniff and pee all you want when we get home."

Home already seemed far away even though we'd only gone a quarter mile or so. I wondered if we could find our way back on our own and even considered that Rocky may have been wise to stay put. I quickly banished the notion by reminding myself that nothing's ever accomplished by staying put.

"Hey, Freddy. How much farther to Chieftess Fox's headquarters?" I asked.

Freddy Fox stopped.

"It's not much farther, Bunny, but it's not much nearer just the same."

I head-butted Lily's shoulder.

"What kind of answer was that?"

"A confusing one, I'd say."

"Should we turn around and head home?"

Part of me hoped Lily would say "Yes"; another part of me felt glad when she said, "No, we'll keep going."

So we continued following Freddy Fox, sometimes on sidewalks, other times cutting through alleys leading between buildings to different streets that looked similar to the one we'd just been on. We soon arrived at a wide river called the Thames, which I recognized from a TV show about cities built on rivers, so people from all over the world could visit them on boats. We stopped beside the water and gazed at the lights on the other side, Goldy's tail wagging so fast that his entire back end wagged along with it.

"Can I go swimming, mum?"

"No, Goldy, you *cannot* go swimming."

Goldy's wagging slowed.

"Can I go swimming another time?"

"Maybe I'll ask your granny and granddad to buy you a wading pool for your first birthday...if you're good, that is."

"Hooray!"

"Shush, Goldy. You have to be quiet."

The river looked so pretty and vibrant with the city lights sparkling off its rippled surface.

"Is Chieftess Fox's headquarters on the other side?" I asked Freddy Fox.

"It is. But don't worry, I know an easy way across, if that's where you want to go."

I nearly said, "Of course, that's where we want to go! What do you think we're doing here?" But I held my tongue, and we resumed trailing the fox while a low-slung barge on the river moved silently along with us.

Before we knew it, Goldy broke free of Lily and began to race the big, flat boat.

"*Goooldy!*" Lily cried.

Goldy returned to us breathing hard, his bubblegum-colored tongue hanging from his mouth.

"Mum, can I ask Freddy Fox if he'll come to the house and play sometime?"

"We have to stay focused on our goal right now, Goldy."

"Okay, I'll stay focused. What was our goal again?"

"Getting to Chieftess Fox's headquarters...and in one piece."

"That's right. I remember now."

Goldy instantly forgot about our goal and charged a seagull balanced on the metal barrier keeping us from falling into the water. The seagull flew away, so Goldy occupied himself by running circles around Freddy Fox.

"Please leave Freddy Fox alone!" Lily said. "This isn't a play date!"

We soon arrived at a bridge extending over the Thames, the famous clock tower named Big Ben standing tall and imposing on the far side of it.

"This is Westminster Bridge," Freddy Fox said.

Goldy's mouth dropped open.

"You mean where the Westminster Dog Show is?"

"The Westminster Dog Show is actually in New York City, where I happened to live, by the way," I said. "How do you know about the Westminster Dog Show, Goldy?"

"I watched it on TV with my granny and granddad," Goldy said. "They told me I could easily win it."

Only if the show had a "Silliest Puppy" category, I thought.

"You probably *could* win it," I said, never one to throw cold water on anyone's dream. "You *are* a special dog."

Freddy Fox guided us onto the bridge and along its walkway.

"Will it be much farther?" Lily called to him. "Not that I'm rushing you!"

Freddy Fox stopped again.

"It's not far once we arrive at our destination. Let's keep moving so we're not spotted out in the open."

Good point. A fox, a girl, a puppy, and a cat crossing Westminster Bridge together after midnight made a strange sight that might prompt someone to call the police. We kept going, and Big Ben and some huge, serious-looking buildings greeted us as we approached the other side. Freddy Fox paused so we could catch up, giving me the chance to ask him some personal questions. One thing I've learned is everyone has a story.

"I was born in Hyde Park two Marches ago," Freddy Fox told me. "March is when many foxes give birth, and lots of cubs are born right in Hyde Park, where we're headed."

"I *love* Hyde Park," Lily said. "You're so lucky to have been born there."

Freddy Fox shrugged.

"I don't know if I'd consider myself lucky. My life's actually been tough so far. The weather isn't always pleasant, I'm frequently short of food, and I'm often dodging cars and people who aren't particularly nice."

"I'm sorry to hear that," I said.

"Believe me, Bunny, most foxes would rather live in the countryside, where there's fresh air to breathe and meadows and woods to run through and lakes and streams to swim in. The problem is there isn't enough countryside left for us now that cities like London have grown so large and the suburbs have spread so much."

I'd had no idea how difficult life could be for foxes. Listening to Freddy Fox reminded me to always see things from the other person's or animal's point of view—to imagine walking a mile in their shoes or on their paws. I felt tempted to tell Freddy Fox about my own rough beginning and how things can get better if you don't lose hope or give up. But the night wasn't about me and my story; it was about Lily and the foxes and even about Goldy, who seemed to be enjoying our journey immensely so far.

"It makes me sad people aren't always nice to you, Freddy Fox," Lily said. "I didn't want to mention this earlier, but maybe it's because some of them believe foxes not only litter the pavements and streets but also threaten their children and pets."

"That's not cool!" Goldy said. "*Not cool at all!*"

"Even if it *is* true, I myself would never threaten a baby or a pet," Freddy Fox said. "None of my friends or family would, either. All babies and pets are so cute and innocent. I mean, just look at Goldy!"

"I might be a pet, but I'm *not* a baby!" Goldy said. "I'm already six months old."

Freddy Fox chuckled before heading off the bridge onto a wide street named Great George that took us past Westminster Palace and the Houses of Parliament, then good, old Big Ben and a statue of a man wearing an overcoat and holding a thin cane. Lily told me the statue depicted Winston Churchill, who once served as England's Prime Minister. A massive government building loomed across Great George Street from Mr. Churchill. I imagined all the long corridors that must be inside the building and wished I could sneak in and run through them. Perhaps I'll do that another time, Dear Reader, and perhaps you'll come with me.

***

We arrived at St. James Park soon after passing the government building. It became darker and spookier in the park, which resembled a jungle in some distant part of the world. St. James has a large pond with an island in it that made me think of Manhattan Island, the part of New York City I lived in before moving to London. Lily became even quieter as she steered her bicycle behind Freddy Fox. I sensed that her courage needed more bolstering...as did my own.

"Hey, Lily. How many apples grow on a tree?

"I don't know. How many apples grow on a tree?"

"All of them!"

"Good riddle, Bunny."

"I don't understand," Goldy said.

Freddy Fox circled back to us.

"Here's a riddle: You must transport a fox, a chicken, and a bag of chicken feed across a river using a boat that's big enough to take only one of them across at a time. You can't leave the fox with the chicken because it might eat the chicken. And you can't leave the chicken with the feed because it might eat the feed. So what do you do?"

Goldy and I were stumped. Not Lily.

"You must take the chicken across first and the feed next," she said. "But instead of leaving the chicken with the feed, you bring it back to the other side, leave it there, and bring the fox across. Then you return for the chicken and bring it across once more. That way, the chicken is never alone with the feed, and the fox is never alone with the chicken."

Freddy Fox looked as stunned as I felt.

"Well done, Lily!" he said. "Just so you know, if *I* was the fox in the riddle, I would never eat the chicken. I'd rather eat leftovers than kill things."

"I'm very confused," Goldy said. "Can I wee now, mum?"

"Wee away, Goldy."

Goldy ran to the nearest tree and began to pee against it. We continued on after he finished, deeper into St. James Park. I soon spotted Buckingham Palace through the trees and recalled reading that the Queen of England lives there.

"Are you sure Chieftess Fox will be at her headquarters?" I called to Freddy Fox.

"She's there ninety-six percent of the time. Or maybe it's ninety-five percent of the time, which is even better."

Ninety-six percent of the time sounded better than ninety-five percent of the time, but I'm no mathematician.

St. James Park soon opened into a large lawn named Green Park, its far end bordered by Piccadilly, a wide, busy street on which cars and big, red double-decker buses zoomed back and forth. We waited for traffic to break before crossing Piccadilly into the much larger Hyde Park. Hyde Park seemed even darker than St. James and Green Park had, and I imagined foxes watching us from behind its many tall trees. I even started to wonder if Freddy Fox had lured us into a trap. But I quickly exchanged those negative, fearful thoughts for positive, logical ones. After all, Freddy Fox had given us no reason to doubt his good intentions. Plus, *we'd* approached *him* about seeing Chieftess Fox, not the other way around.

The darkness and quiet thickened as we ventured into the heart of Hyde Park. An owl's hooting broke the silence, and I noticed bats swooping like ghost shadows through the night sky. Goldy stuck by our side now, and Lily stayed close behind Freddy Fox, as if she feared losing him.

Freddy Fox finally stopped.

"We're here," he said.

"Here" didn't appear to be anywhere at all. I'd been expecting a palace like Westminster or Buckingham. No palace in sight. Nor a mansion, or a house, or even a cottage.

"This is Chieftess Fox's headquarters?" Lily asked.

"It is, indeed," Freddy Fox answered.

"I don't see any headquarters," I said, trying to disguise my disappointment.

"Just because something isn't there doesn't mean it's not there," Freddy Fox said.

He then started scratching at what looked like a large, flat rock that turned out to be a wooden plank. The plank moved to the side, and the head of another fox emerged from the hole it had been concealing. The fox's eyes shifted this way and that until they eventually settled on Lily.

"Who's the girl?" he asked Freddy Fox.

"Her name's Lily Hayward, and she's a friend of mine."

The fox looked at Goldy.

"What about the little yellow dog?"

"Goldy won't cause any trouble," Freddy Fox said. "At least not the troublesome kind."

The fox looked at me next.

"How about the cat with the green eyes and pointy ears?"

"Bunny?" Freddy Fox said. "Bunny happens to be the coolest cat I've ever met."

The fox pondered this.

"I'll take your word for it. What do they want?"

"To meet Chieftess."

"To meet Chieftess? You don't just *meet* Chieftess Fox. Why?"

"To see if they can find a way to prevent the fox cull the humans are cooking up."

I felt sure the fox in the hole would turn us away then. Instead, a twinkle replaced the suspicion clouding his eyes.

"Why didn't you say so in the first place, Freddy?" he asked. "They may enter, but just so you know, they might never come out again."

That's exactly what I *didn't* want to hear. The fox ducked back into the hole before I could demand he clarify the "never coming out" part of his statement.

"Are we supposed to go down there?" Lily asked, sounding as tentative as I felt.

Freddy Fox nodded and said, "Don't worry—it's actually quite safe...in a relative manner."

"Maybe for foxes," I said.

"I've dug holes in the garden," Goldy said. "But *never* one like this."

Lily took a deep breath and let it out slowly.

"Okay, we'll go into the hole," she said, without much conviction.

With that, she dismounted her bicycle and leaned it against a tree. She tightened the straps of the knapsack and crouched before Goldy.

"You're to stay with me at all times, little boy," she said, shaking her finger inches from his snout. "No matter what happens. Understood?"

"Understood! *Understood!*"

"Are you guys ready?" Freddy Fox asked.

"I think so," Lily said.

Freddy Fox smiled and slithered into the hole the way water flows into a drain. But Lily didn't follow him; she instead remained perfectly still, staring into the dark abyss that could have led to the fiery center of the earth for all we knew. In those silent, fateful moments, I pressed my ear to Lily's back and heard her heart beating fast and loud. *Boom-boom, boom-boom, boom-boom.* I felt my own heart beating just as hard. And for moments that felt like hours, I imagined that her heart and mine had joined and were beating as one.

CHAPTER 5

DOWN INTO CHIEFTESS FOX'S HEADQUARTERS

Lily stood there in the middle of Hyde Park, in the middle of that dark, hushed night, seemingly paralyzed by the prospect of going into the hole Freddy Fox had just slipped into. I searched for the right words to get her moving.

"We've come all this way, Lily," was all I could think of.

That's all I needed, as it turned out. Lily gathered Goldy in her arms; she then dipped her right foot into the hole, as if testing the temperature of the water in a swimming pool. She placed her left foot in next, and, to my surprise, she kept going into what became a narrow tunnel with jagged granite walls. Cold water dripped on us from the low ceiling, and a moldy odor filled my nostrils. The blackness in the tunnel became even blacker as it angled downward. Thankfully, Freddy Fox's claws scratching the rocky floor made enough noise for us to track him.

"How much deeper does it go?" Lily said, her voice echoing.

"Only a little deeper than the bottom," Freddy Fox's voice echoed back.

I wondered how it could possibly go any deeper than the bottom.

"I have to wee again, mum," Goldy said.

"Can you hold it, Goldy?"

"I think so."

I heard whizzing seconds later, followed by the unmistakable scent of puppy pee.

"Oh, Goldy."

"Sorry, mum."

We stayed with Freddy Fox, and I felt a little better when a flickering orange light appeared ahead. The light gradually brightened as we moved toward it, and the tunnel soon opened into a ginormous cavern lit by fire torches protruding from holes in its walls.

Mewow!

Hundreds of scurrying foxes filled the cavern, reminding me of a swarming beehive I'd once seen on a TV nature show. The frenetic activity ceased the moment the foxes noticed us; hundreds of canine eyes suddenly trained on none other than Lily, Goldy, and me. It became quiet enough to hear the water drip, drip, dripping from above.

Lily stopped and stood nearly as still as the statue of Winston Churchill we'd passed earlier. I leaned forward again until my whiskers tickled her left earlobe.

"Hey, Lily. Why did the chicken cross the road?" I whispered.

"Another riddle with a chicken in it, Bunny?" Lily whispered back.

"I happen to like riddles with chickens in them."

"Everyone knows the chicken crossed the road to get to the other side."

The super-easy riddle seemed to irritate Lily, but also eased some of her fear.

"I'll take you to Chieftess Fox now," Freddy Fox said.

"Will she be expecting us?" Lily asked.

Freddy Fox shrugged.

"She might be, although she has no idea you're actually here."

"I'll do the talking, if you want," I said to Lily, ignoring Freddy Fox's nonsensical statement.

"Thanks, Bunny, but I think I can handle it."

That's the spirit, Lily Hayward!

We followed Freddy Fox through the sea of foxes that closed in behind us like the jaws of a huge beast. Freddy Fox led us to a smaller cave extending off the main cavern. He pulled aside a scrap of carpet hung over the cave entrance and exchanged muffled words with its occupant.

"She says to come in," he said, turning to us.

Freddy Fox ushered us into the cave, and there, on a ledge carved into its wall, sat the one and only Chieftess Fox! The leader of the London foxes looked much like the others—roughly the same size and shape and color. The only noticeable difference was her eyes; a patch similar to those worn by pirates covered one of them.

"I am Chieftess Fox," she said in a harsh-sounding tone, her exposed eye giving us a hard stare.

I heard Lily swallow what must have felt like a lump in her throat.

"How do you do, Chieftess Fox? I'm Lily Hayward, the cat in my knapsack is Bunny, and this is Goldy."

Chieftess Fox glowered down at us.

"Freddy Fox already told me your names. Now, why are you here?"

"First of all, I want to thank you for allowing us into your headquarters," Lily said. "It's quite an honor."

"Correction: I didn't *allow* you into my headquarters. You came without an invitation."

Lily's breathing suddenly became quick and shallow, and much of the color had drained from her cheeks.

"That's true, but— "

"I wouldn't come into *your* house without an invitation," Chieftess Fox interrupted. "Very rude, which is to be expected of humans, I suppose."

"I'm sorry, Chieftess Fox," Lily said. "Coming here was my idea, so please don't blame Goldy or Bunny. And our intentions are good, if you'll let me explain them."

I noticed four fierce-looking foxes had blocked the entrance of the cave, eliminating any chance of escape.

"I'm in no mood for explanations," Chieftess Fox said, her eye darkening along with her mood. "Humans talk and talk and talk, but most of their words are meaningless and can't be trusted."

I began to squirm in the knapsack—my way of telling Lily to let me out. She did, and it sure felt good to stretch my legs and arch my back. I wouldn't have minded a runaround followed by an ear scratch and a nice belly rub. Chieftess Fox glared at me while suppressing what looked like a smirk.

"You sure are a small cat," she said.

I glared and smirked right back at her.

"I might be small, but I wouldn't underestimate me."

"Are you challenging me, Bunny? *In my own headquarters?*"

"I could ask you the same thing," I said, unsure if that made any sense, trying to sound brave nonetheless.

Goldy had sprawled on the floor of the cave during this tense exchange, his paws folded over his eyes and across the bridge of his snout. I think I even heard him whimpering. Lily looked as pale as a sheet by then, and the foxes in the entrance appeared to be awaiting Chieftess Fox's signal to pounce. I knew I had to do something fast and recalled reading that the best defense is often a good offense. I hopped onto the ledge beside Chieftess Fox with this in mind.

"Tell me what happened to your eye, Chieftess Fox," I said.

"Why do you want to know?"

"I'm curious."

"Why do you even care?"

"Because I'm a caring cat. Are you going to tell me?"

Chieftess Fox glanced at the fierce-looking foxes, and I felt sure she would order them to devour us at any moment. I don't think I've ever felt so frightened, and I mustered every ounce of strength not to show it. Chieftess Fox turned to me.

"If you must know, I lost it to a bullet four years ago when I lived in the countryside. A human shot at me, and I'm lucky I only lost an eye that day."

"That's awful," I said.

Chieftess Fox aimed an accusatory look at Goldy.

"A human took my eye, but not without the help of dogs who assisted by chasing and cornering me."

Goldy lifted his head from beneath his paws.

"Wait, whaaat? *Dogs?*"

"A different breed than you, but dogs regardless."

Goldy seemed stricken.

"I'm sorry, Chieftess Fox. Foxes are my cousins, and all I want to do is play with them."

I looked at Lily, glad to see some color had returned to her cheeks and some resolve to her eyes.

"I understand the reasons you don't like us," Lily said. "But we've traveled a long way tonight, and I believe that gives us the right to tell you why."

"Very well," Chieftess Fox said. "Make it fast, though. I'm busy. It's not easy being in charge of so many foxes."

She dropped down from the ledge, and the four of us sat in a circle on the rug covering the cave floor.

"We're here because we're concerned about the upcoming fox cull," Lily said.

Chieftess Fox seemed skeptical.

"Isn't killing foxes what you humans enjoy most?"

"Actually, the majority of humans genuinely like foxes," Lily said.

"I find that hard to believe."

"It's true, Chieftess Fox."

"Can't everyone just play together?" Goldy said.

In the silence that followed, my spirits sank with the realization that we'd made the long trek to Hyde Park with no specific plan to prevent the cull.

"It might help if the foxes didn't make such a mess with the garbage," I said, hoping to get the conversation started again.

Chieftess Fox frowned at me.

"My foxes need to eat, Bunny. Much of our natural territory in the countryside's been taken from us. That leaves us little choice but to scavenge for food here in the city."

"Fair enough," I said. "What about reports of foxes threatening children and pets?"

"If that's true, it will stop immediately," Chieftess Fox said. "I'll issue a decree to all my foxes this very night."

"That would be much appreciated," Lily said.

Chieftess Fox sat up straighter.

"While it's important for foxes to understand humans' concerns, it's equally important for humans to understand ours. Besides crowding foxes out of their natural habitat, humans have been hunting them for hundreds of years. For sport and fun—not even for food!"

"Isn't fox hunting in England illegal now?" Lily said.

"Some humans do it anyway, as my missing eye clearly illustrates. And I've heard even more humans want to make it legal again."

Lily went into a deep think.

"How about separate food bins?" she said, emerging from it.

Chieftess Fox seemed perplexed.

"Separate food bins?"

I felt as perplexed as Chieftess Fox looked—that is until I recalled Rocky mentioning separate food bins the previous day in the brief gap between his naps.

"That's right," Lily continued. "What if humans started putting their food waste in separate bins foxes could access without tipping them over?"

Chieftess Fox mulled Lily's suggestion.

"Not a bad idea."

"And maybe if foxes are tidier and they help humans dispose of their food garbage, humans wouldn't have to spend so much time and money cleaning it up and carting it away to landfills that take up more fox territory," I said, breathless from speaking that long sentence without a pause.

"That would also be good for the environment," Lily added.

"It all makes perfect sense in theory," Chieftess Fox said. "My question is, 'How would it happen in reality?'"

"Not to worry, Chieftess Fox," Lily said, her confidence growing. "Bunny, Goldy, and I will figure it out. You just need to determine if your foxes would agree to such an arrangement."

Chieftess Fox thought for nearly a full minute this time.

"There shall be a referendum on it tomorrow night," she finally declared.

I knew from the dictionary that "referendum" meant "vote."

"We'll be here for it," I said.

"Excellent! Now you three best get home before your parents wake and discover you're gone."

"Good idea," Lily said. "None of this will work if we get grounded."

Being grounded would, indeed, have been the last thing we needed. So we stood and started toward the cave entrance, still blocked by the four menacing foxes.

"*Stop right there!*" Chieftess Fox said after we'd gone only a few steps.

We stopped and faced Chieftess Fox again, her eye trained only on me now.

"Is everything okay?" I asked.

"Something's been bothering me ever since you arrived, Bunny. I know you, don't I?"

"I believe tonight's the first time we've ever met."

"True, but I know you from somewhere." Recognition flickered into her eye then. "Hey, aren't you the cat who saved the Central Park carriage horse in New York City last year?"

"That would be me," I said, trying my best to sound modest.

"What an incredible feat."

"No big deal, really."

"Oh, but it was. *A very big deal!*"

"I just try to help. You could say it's my thing."

"You don't just *try* to help, Bunny—you *succeed!*"

Chieftess Fox smiled for the first time since we'd arrived. She then wished us a safe trip, and off we went, up through the tunnel and out the hole into Hyde Park. Lily put me back in the knapsack, retrieved her bicycle, and the three of us started the long trek home through the London night, this time without Freddy Fox to guide us.

CHAPTER 6

THE VOTE AND THE SOCCER GAME

We managed to make it home from Chieftess Fox's headquarters all by ourselves. More importantly, our parents never discovered we'd even been gone! We met in Lily's garden the next night and were pleased to find Freddy Fox waiting outside Lily's house.

"Nice of you to come for us, Freddy Fox," I said.

"You really didn't have to," Lily said.

Freddy Fox seemed as pleased to see us as we were to see him.

"It's my pleasure. Besides, Chieftess Fox wanted to make absolutely sure you're there for the big vote."

"We wouldn't miss it for the world," Lily said.

"You could offer me a whole bag of puppy treats, and I still wouldn't miss it!" Goldy said.

It didn't seem to take as long to get to Chieftess Fox's headquarters this time, and even more foxes filled the cavern than the previous night. Freddy Fox escorted us through them to Chieftess Fox's cave.

"I'm very pleased you returned," Chieftess Fox said, beaming at us from her ledge.

"We said we would," Lily said. "We always keep our word."

Goldy jumped onto the ledge beside Chieftess Fox.

"Can I ask you a small question, Chieftess Fox?"

"Sure, Goldy."

"Are there any fox puppies I can play with?"

"There are, but we have to do the referendum first."

"What's a 'referendum,' again?"

"A referendum is a vote on a particular issue. Tonight all the London foxes will be voting on whether to eat only out of separate food bins."

"What about not harming children and pets?" Lily said.

Chieftess Fox gave Lily a resolute stare that I mistook for an angry one at first.

"Lily, I *promise* no London fox will ever threaten or harm a child or pet."

Good old Chieftess Fox!

She came down from the ledge, and the four of us filed out of the cave into the cavern, which had become packed with even more foxes. We followed Chieftess Fox through the furry throng to the center, where she climbed onto a boulder, aimed her snout toward the ceiling, and let out a series of high-pitched barks.

"Ow-wow-wow-wow-wow!"

The cavern instantly silenced, and all fox eyes immediately shifted to Chieftess Fox, who introduced Lily, me, and Goldy before explaining the reason for the referendum. Whispers and murmurs rippled through the foxes, and I worried they might be planning to vote *against* using separate food bins and *against* being tidy and even against not harming children and pets.

Chieftess Fox issued another series of lower-pitched barks, and what followed is one of the most amazing sights I've ever seen—hundreds of foxes rearing onto their hind legs while raising their front paws into the air and howling at the top of their lungs. *Mewow!* The sight of them upright and howling all at once is something I'll never forget.

Chieftess Fox looked down at us once the foxes returned to all fours and quieted.

"There you have it. My foxes have voted to accept your plan."

I gazed up at Lily and saw a big smile spreading across her face. I smiled, too, which cats normally don't do. Although we hadn't yet stopped the fox cull or solved the garbage problem, I'd say we'd made a good start. Which meant it was time to celebrate!

And there's no better way to do that than with an impromptu game of soccer—or "football," as the English call it. One of the foxes produced a dirty, scuffed-up ball.

"We shall now play a game of footy to commemorate this historic agreement between the humans and foxes of London!" Chieftess Fox proclaimed.

I had neither the heart nor the nerve to remind Chieftess Fox that only the foxes had agreed to their end of the deal—that Lily and Goldy and I still had to convince Londoners to actually use separate food bins.

"We're going to play now?" Goldy said, his tail wagging so fast it had become a blur.

"Yes, Goldy," Lily said. "Not the kind of play you do in the garden, mind you. This type has rules and an objective."

"What's an 'objective,' mum?"

"In this case, it's to score more goals than the opposing team. You'll get the hang of it...*if* they let you participate."

Being the smallest creature there, I wasn't sure *I* should participate. I had little choice, as it turned out. Two teams were formed by dividing the cavern in half; one team occupying one end, the other team occupying the other. Spectators crowded the sides, and the goalkeepers created goalposts by placing empty soup cans on the cavern floor. Chieftess Fox then let out a shrill *Yip! Yip! Yip!*, and the game began.

***

Foxes converged on the ball from all directions. I moved to the sideline to avoid being trampled. Goldy, on the other hand, joined right in, chasing the ball rolling back and forth and from side to side

as foxes frantically batted it with their paws. Lily acted more like a spectator than a player, but only until the ball happened to come right to her. She unleashed a big kick that sent it flying. Lily had officially entered the game! Goldy ran after the ball Lily had kicked and somehow managed to get to it before any of the foxes! But instead of swatting the ball toward the goal, the tiny dog pounced on it and immediately rolled off onto his back, his paws momentarily pointing upward. He righted himself and then started swatting the ball toward our goal instead of the opposing team's.

"You're going the wrong way, Goldy!" his teammates cried. *"Go toward the other goal!"*

Goldy had become too caught up in the moment to hear them, his brow furrowed with determination as his stubby legs propelled him and the ball toward the wrong goal. Fortunately for his team, Goldy's legs were moving so fast he tripped and rolled into a triple somersault. He sprang back onto his paws after his tumble and continued chasing the ball, still with no apparent idea what to do with it.

The game went on for what seemed like a long time; there was still no score and the foxes were panting harder and harder with each passing minute. Then, unexpectedly, the ball came directly to me. I discarded my caution and smacked it with my paw. The ball miraculously shot to none other than Lily, who quickly pivoted and kicked as hard as she could. The ball flew from her foot toward the opposing goal and, at the last moment, bounced up and over the keeper's reaching paws. It came down behind him and skittered between the soup cans.

Goooooaal!

Lily raised her arms and began to jump up and down. Her fox teammates gathered around her, gleefully yipping and yowling and barking. I'd never seen Lily look so happy, which made me equally happy! Goldy broke into a dance, swishing his tail and tapping his paws against the ground. I couldn't help dancing myself, shaking my butt and bobbing my head. I imagine I looked just as funny as Goldy did!

The game finally ended in a 1-1 draw, all the player and spectator foxes giving each other hugs and high-fives afterward. Some even gave Lily and Goldy and me hugs and high-fives, too! I felt as if we'd made hundreds of new friends and had so much fun doing it. Not to mention getting a serious workout.

The three of us would have rested after the game had we not needed to get home before our parents woke. So we said goodbye to Chieftess Fox and Freddy Fox and all our new fox friends before climbing out of the cavern back into Hyde Park, which seemed especially quiet after the boisterous gathering we'd been part of beneath it.

"I must say, I'm knackered," Lily said.

"Me, too," I said.

Goldy flopped on his belly, each leg splayed in a different direction. "I'm pooped!"

Lily reclaimed her bicycle from beside the tree, put me back in the knapsack, and together we trudged through the park until we reached Piccadilly. I spotted a double-decker bus with "Lambeth" written on its front as we waited to cross the street.

"Hey, Lily. Let's get on that bus and take it home to Lambeth."

Lily seemed hesitant.

"Do you think the driver will allow a bicycle, a puppy, and a cat on?"

"Normally, no, but it's late, and he might make an exception."

We got to the stop just as the bus pulled up. The driver opened the door and looked down at us with a stern expression.

"Tell him we're lost and need to get home," I whispered to Lily.

Lily did, but the driver shook his head.

"No cats or bicycles allowed," he said. "And dogs are permitted only at my discretion."

While I desperately searched for a way to convince the driver to disregard the rules, Goldy took it upon himself to yank the leash from Lily's hand, bound up the bus steps, and jump right onto his lap! Goldy started licking the driver's face, and the man's resolve quickly

crumbled before Goldy's cuteness assault. The driver began to laugh so hard he couldn't speak, which left him no choice but to wave us into the bus. He even refused to take Lily's money. We thanked him before climbing the stairs to the top level.

Luckily, the front seats were unoccupied—not that we sat in them for long. Too much to look at! Lily took me out of the knapsack and pressed her nose to the window. I stood on my hind legs next to her, and Goldy propped his paws against the glass on my other side, his mouth partially open. "Oooh, look at that, mum! Oooh, look at this, mum!" he'd say whenever we passed something that interested him, which included pretty much everything. I knew how he felt, having been equally mesmerized by New York City when my friend Peter the Deliveryman had taken me to Central Park in the basket of his bicycle.

Oh, what a wonderful nighttime ride through London we had, passing the palaces and government buildings and Houses of Parliament we'd seen on our way to Hyde Park! We passed Big Ben again and Churchill, too. This time I noticed a giant Ferris wheel beside the Thames and made a mental note to go on it some day. I looked down at the water as we went over Westminster Bridge and imagined the double-decker had become an ocean liner taking us to some faraway port.

"Can we stay on this bus for a long time, mum?" Goldy asked.

I felt the same way, but knew we'd be in big trouble if we didn't get home soon.

"We'll go on one again another time," Lily said.

"Can Bunny come with us when we do?"

"Invitation accepted, Goldy," I said.

The bus took us to the other side of Westminster and along the south bank of the Thames toward Lambeth. I wondered where the river would lead if I rode a boat all the way to its end, but I realized that would have to be part of another adventure. We still had much to do in this one!

The bus turned after going roughly half a mile. It followed a familiar-looking street away from the river and soon pulled to the curb only two blocks from our houses. We dashed down the steps when we heard the bus doors open, making sure to thank the driver again on our way out. The man smiled and waved to us before driving off, leaving us on the sidewalk, feeling tired but excited and hopeful.

Lily mounted her bicycle and pedaled the rest of the way while Goldy jogged beside us. We snuck through the gate into Lily's yard and found Rocky sleeping on the wall, right where we'd left him. I don't think he'd moved an inch!

Rocky opened only one eye.

"How'd everything go?"

Lily started telling him about our return to Chieftess Fox's headquarters and the referendum and the soccer game and the double-decker ride home. But the big cat fell asleep again halfway through Lily's story. He even began to snore!

"Hey, Bunny?" Goldy said.

"Yes, Goldy?"

"Can we play a little bit?"

"We'll play tomorrow. It's bedtime now."

Goldy clearly didn't want our big night to end.

"Maybe some of the foxes will come over and play with us," he said.

"You never know, Goldy."

Lily freed me from the knapsack and then went inside with her puppy. I jumped over the wall into my own yard and tiptoed into my house. In the kitchen, I noticed a copy of *The Guardian* newspaper on the table, its front page featuring an article about something called the Mayor's Annual Children's Choice Letter Contest. I read the entire piece despite my fatigue, and learned all about the competition in which children write to the Mayor of London with solutions to various problems the city faces. The mayor chooses one such letter each year and implements its suggestion. The deadline for this year's contest happened to be less than a week away!

I climbed the stairs to Joan's and Robert's room afterward. Both my parents were sleeping as soundly as Rocky had been, so I crept like a ninja into their bed and curled up in the "power alley" between them. But I couldn't sleep. I instead tossed and turned and fidgeted for hours, all the while thinking about the impending Mayor's Annual Children's Choice Letter Contest.

CHAPTER 7

LETTER TO THE MAYOR

Lily sat at her desk and wrote the following letter to the Mayor of London, with my input, of course.

Dear Mr. Mayor,

My name is Lily Hayward. I'm ten years old, and I live in Lambeth. I have two nice parents and a golden labrador puppy named Goldy, who can be a handful at times. I like to read and play with Goldy in the garden. I also enjoy eating ice cream and riding my bicycle.

I'm entering the Mayor's Annual Children's Choice Letter Contest because of something concerning to me and my friends. That happens to be the fox cull being planned here in London. We're upset by the cull because we think foxes are lovely creatures that mean no harm despite what some people believe. In fact, they're only trying to get enough to eat. We've actually learned the main reason so many foxes are in London is because much of their natural habitat in the countryside has been replaced by houses and shops and roads and car parks. This forces them to come to the city to find food, which causes the problem of foxes tipping over rubbish bins to get at what's inside, creating a right mess in the process.

My friend, Bunny, once told me there's a solution to every problem. Bunny and I happen to believe a solution to the problem of foxes littering London's pavements and streets would be to provide special rubbish bins just for food waste. The bins would be lower than the

regular ones so foxes could access them without toppling them. The bins could also have special lids that allow foxes to push their snouts in while keeping out rats and bugs and flies. Speaking of rats and bugs and flies, we believe there would be fewer of them once people start using the bins because less food scraps would be scattered about. Finally, because foxes could eat our food waste more easily, the city would spend less money cleaning it up and hauling it away. Better for the environment, too!

We think our idea is fairly easy to do and might keep our city cleaner, save money and the environment and, best of all, make a mean, nasty fox cull unnecessary.

Please consider our idea for your contest, Mr. Mayor. We think it would be good for London and its residents and, just as importantly, for our friends the foxes. We also think it's the compassionate thing to do.

Thanks very much for reading my letter and for being my mayor.

Respectfully,

Lily Hayward

I went with Lily to the mailbox later that day and we dropped the letter into it.

Then we waited.

LILY HAYWARD

CHAPTER 8

AND THE WINNER IS...

More than a week passed after Lily and I wrote to the London mayor. During that time, I kept so busy exploring the house and yard, sleeping, scratching furniture, and cuddling with mom and dad, that I forgot all about the letter. Then came the morning I wandered into the kitchen and found Robert at the table reading *The Guardian* newspaper while Joan sat across from him, staring at her smartphone thing. I crouched on the floor and looked up at my parents with my best "Can I have treats?" expression on my face. Joan and Robert seemed too absorbed in reading to even notice me.

Robert finally looked up from the newspaper, thought crinkling his brow.

"Hey, isn't Lily Hayward the girl who lives next door?"

Joan pulled her eyes from her phone.

"I believe she is. She seems like very a nice girl."

"Well, she not only seems very nice, she also seems very clever. I'm reading here her letter won the Mayor's Annual Children's Choice Letter Contest."

Joan started pushing on her phone with her thumbs, then moving her index finger along the screen.

"Incredible," she said, squinting at it. "I wonder how such a young girl came up with such an ingenious plan."

"Do you think it will work?" Robert said.

"I don't see why not. I'll make sure we get a separate food bin as soon as they're available."

I maintained an impassive cat face while summoning every ounce of willpower to keep from telling them that Lily, Goldy, I, and even Rocky, had made it all happen. I restrained the urge to tell them about our adventures with Freddy Fox and Chieftess Fox and the hundreds of others beneath Hyde Park. Because doing so would also be admitting to breaking the promise I'd made after saving Joe the Carriage Horse in New York City last year, *the one to behave and stay out of trouble*. I knew telling mom and dad would almost certainly mean being confined to the house from then on, which would *also* mean not seeing Lily and Goldy and Rocky anymore. So I kept my mouth shut and went out into the yard, where I found Rocky on the wall, wide awake, for a change. I told Rocky about the separate-food-bin proposal and even had to remind him *he'd* thought of it in the first place.

"They should have separate food bins for cats, too," Rocky said. "I'm tired of waiting around to be fed."

"You *do* realize you'd have to retrieve meals from the bin yourself, Rocky."

Rocky contemplated that, but only briefly.

"On second thought, I'm good the way things are."

Goldy burst out of the Hayward house and pranced over to the wall before I could tease Rocky about his laziness.

"Hi, Goldy. Where's Lily?"

"She's in the loo, so I snuck out. Please don't tell granny and granddad."

"I won't, you mischievous puppy."

A sleepy-eyed, tussle-haired Lily emerged moments later.

"Did you hear the news, Lily?" I said.

"What news?"

I felt glad my friend hadn't yet heard she'd won the Mayor's Annual Children's Choice Letter Contest. That meant I got to be the one to tell her! When I did, she smiled even more brightly than she had after scoring the soccer goal. She promptly gave me and Goldy big hugs, and tears had replaced her smile by the time she released us.

"Are you okay, Lily?"

Lily dabbed her eyes with a tissue.

"*Am I okay?* I don't think I've ever been better."

Goldy's tail had started wagging in circles, like a helicopter blade.

"Guess what, Bunny?"

"What?"

"It's time to play!"

"Okay, Goldy. Let's play."

Goldy and I began to run around Lily's yard. Goldy chased me. Then I chased him. Then we wrestled and rolled about until we were both completely spent. We rested on the patch of grass beside Mrs. Hayward's tulips and soon fell asleep. And while Goldy probably dreamt of butterflies and birds and soccer balls and foxes, I dreamt about what would happen next now that the mayor had chosen Lily's letter for the Mayor's Annual Children's Choice Letter Contest.

***

I had to wait nearly a month to find out; a month that seemed more like eternity for a young critter like me. Then, finally, the big day arrived. Lily insisted Goldy and I accompany her to the ceremony at London City Hall, during which the mayor dedicated a special food

bin to kick off the initiative. Lily had invited Rocky as well, but Rocky had declined, explaining he had too many things to do in the garden.

Goldy and I, on the other hand, were delighted to go! I mean, how often do you get to be on TV? Actually, I *was* on TV last year, saving Joe the Carriage Horse in New York City. You can even find footage online of me driving Joe's carriage down Fifth Avenue. So there we were, up on stage in London City Hall, surrounded by hundreds of people, some holding cameras and microphones. Lights as hot and bright as summer sun puddles shined right on us.

The mayor seemed like a tough, no-nonsense type of man. I imagine you *have* to be to run a major city like London. But he smiled and his dark eyes softened whenever he looked down at Lily and Goldy and me. He positioned Lily directly in front of him before lifting and tucking me and Goldy beneath each arm like two American footballs. He then said the following into the microphone:

"Thank you for coming, ladies and gentlemen. As you may know, the Mayor's Annual Children's Choice Letter Contest is something I've always been incredibly excited about and proud of. Not only because it engages our youngest citizens, who will lead this city into the future, but because it taps into a wellspring of fresh ideas, into new and creative ways of addressing problems that might seem unsolvable. 'Unsolvable problems.' I believe those two words should never be spoken in the same sentence. To paraphrase the late, great Beatle, John Lennon, as well as the great young lady sharing the stage with me today, there *are* no problems, only solutions. Now, we have to keep this ceremony brief so this extraordinary girl doesn't miss too much school. So without further delay, I'll relinquish the microphone to this year's solutionist so she can explain the problem she identified and her plan to fix it, a plan the city will follow to the best of its ability. Ladies and gentlemen, please give a warm welcome to London's own *Lily Hayward!*"

The crowd applauded as the mayor lowered the microphone to Lily's mouth, then stepped away from it, still holding me and Goldy. Lily now stood alone at center stage in her pretty polka-dot skirt. A long time seemed to pass before she finally cleared her throat and spoke:

"Umm, before I talk about my letter to the mayor regarding the foxes and the rubbish on the pavements and streets, I just want to say I could never have come up with the idea for it—and there would be little chance of the idea actually working—if not for Bunny here and my puppy Goldy and my own cat Rocky, who, unfortunately, couldn't

attend today. I can't ask for better, more loyal friends, and I truly wouldn't have been able to do it without them..."

A big, long car took us from City Hall to a TV station after Lily's City Hall speech. Lily was interviewed on a morning program there while Goldy and I sat on the studio couch beside her, having been treated to thorough brushings beforehand. Lily's teacher asked her to bring me and Goldy to school the next day, and I noticed that the kids who'd once teased Lily now treated her with kindness and respect. Lily had clearly become somewhat of a hero to them, not that she acted like one. Even after all that had happened, she remained the same unassuming soul I've always known, though one who no longer seemed so tentative and unsure of herself. The school principal even convened a special assembly in Lily's honor. Naturally, Goldy began running around the auditorium during it, much to the delight of the students.

We spent the rest of the afternoon at school with Lily and walked home with her when her last class ended. But as the excitement of the previous two days subsided, I started to feel uneasy again. I didn't know why at first. It then dawned on me that, despite all the praise and honors we'd received for coming up with a way to stop the fox cull while keeping the streets of London clean and saving the city money, we still had no idea if it would actually work.

CHAPTER 9

SUCCESS!

"Success" is the word everyone used to describe Lily's food-bin program after it had been in effect for a whole month. By "everyone," I mean the mayor and citizens of London, also newspapers and radio and TV shows, even blogs and all kinds of social media. The program worked mainly because the London foxes had kept their promise to eat only out of the new bins people had started to use.

The fox cull plans stopped as a result. *Officially cancelled!*

The mayor deemed the cull unnecessary, and few disagreed with him. The mayor also declared an end to the food-bin trial period and signed an ordinance making it permanent. I'm happy to report that nearly every house and building in London now has one of Lily's special bins, and almost no trash can be seen on the sidewalks or in the streets. Not to mention that reports of foxes menacing children and pets have completely stopped.

Lily's life has mainly returned to normal, aside from doing the occasional interview. She now has lots of friends at school, and she smiles much more often than she used to. I've even noticed a difference in her eyes; contentment and confidence have replaced the sadness and anxiety that had once filled them. Nothing could make me happier.

Things are pretty much the same for me and Goldy, not that I'm complaining. We happily spend most of our days in the Haywards' yard, either playing tag or batting one of Goldy's tennis balls back and forth between us. I nap when I tire, while Goldy usually keeps going, chasing birds and butterflies and his own tail when he can't find anything else to chase. Rocky still spends the majority of his time sleeping in the plum tree or on the wall. The only difference is he's started wearing an eye mask so he can sleep better on sunny days. He claims to be testing it before selling one to every cat in England and donating the profits to charity.

"Sounds like a good idea, Rocky," I said to him the other day. "How are you going to sell them to other cats?"

"I'm not sure yet, but I'm gonna sell thousands."

"I have no doubt. Which charity do you plan to donate the profits to, if you don't mind me asking?"

Rocky hemmed and hawed.

"I'll find one—don't you worry."

"Let me know if you need any help, Rocky."

"Oh, I will, Bunny."

That night I snuggled in the power alley between Joan and Robert and immediately fell asleep. But a noise out in the street soon woke me. I quietly jumped off the bed and crept to the window. I hopped onto the sill, looked down to the sidewalk, and who did I see beneath the street lamp eating from the special bin Robert had placed in front of the house? Freddy Fox is who! I tapped the window with my paw until Freddy Fox looked up and spotted me. He smiled and wagged his bushy tail. So nice to see my good pal again!

I waved at Freddy Fox before returning to the bed and nestling between Joan and Robert. I don't recall every detail of the dream I soon drifted into, only that it took me to a different city in a different country where Robert had been posted for his diplomat job. There I'd embarked on a whole new adventure with a whole new set of friends, ones I cherished just as much as those I'd made in New York and London. I woke in the morning feeling rested and happy, wondering if my dream would actually come true. You never know, Dear Reader, but I have a feeling it will someday, and someday soon. When it does, I'll be sure to tell you all about it.

WHY KINDNESS MATTERS

In *Hello, My Name is Bunny! London,* Bunny demonstrates at least five ways to lead a kinder, more fulfilled life.

1. Helping others has benefits beyond your original intention. It can lead to new friendships, new opportunities, and an awesome sense of well-being.
2. Take time to understand someone else's perspective. You'll break down barriers and forge new friendships.
3. Encourage your friends when times are tough. A cup half full is always more productive than a cup half empty.
4. Celebrate your friends' successes and achievements with heart-felt congratulations. It will mean the world to them.
5. Always look for ways to pay forward your good fortune with a kind act or word. It feels good and you'll help make the world a better place.

What do you do to live a kind life?

ABOUT THE AUTHORS

Bunny Doogle Simmons-Bloom was born in a basement in Bushwick, Brooklyn, and now lives in the Hudson Valley, NY. Besides writing and reading, Bunny loves to eat, sleep, snuggle, and play. This is Bunny's second book in the *Hello, My Name is Bunny!* series.

Matt Bloom, who helped Bunny write this book, is an adult and children's author. He lives in the Hudson Valley, NY with his wife, Shelley Simmons-Bloom, and Bunny. His children's books are *Hello, My Name is Bunny! New York City* (2016), *Hello, My Name is Bunny! London* (2018), and *Hello, My Name is Bunny! Paris* (2022). Matt has earned fiction fellowships at Sewanee Writers' Conference, Breadloaf Writers' Conference, and a residence at MacDowell Artists' Colony.

All books are available at **www.hellobunnybloom.com**

CPSIA information can be obtained
at www.ICGtesting.com
Printed in the USA
LVHW011930090623
749359LV00011B/179

9 780997 642544